To Wilbur Henry Peter Rowley.
Soon may you hop and bop, T. M.

For Harper, G. P-R.

ORCHARD BOOKS
First published in Great Britain in 2016 by The Watts Publishing Group
This edition first published in 2016
1 3 5 7 9 10 8 6 4 2
Text © Tony Mitton 2016
Illustrations © Guy Parker Rees 2016
The moral rights of the author and illustrator have been asserted.
All rights reserved.
A CIP catalogue record for this book is available from the British Library.
ISBN 978 1 40833 687 8
Printed and bound in China

Orchard Books
An imprint of Hachette Children's Group
Part of The Watts Publishing Group Limited
Carmelite House
50 Victoria Embankment
London EC4Y 0DZ

An Hachette UK Company
www.hachette.co.uk
www.hachettechildrens.co.uk

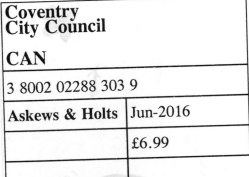
MIX
Paper from
responsible sources
FSC
www.fsc.org
FSC® C104740

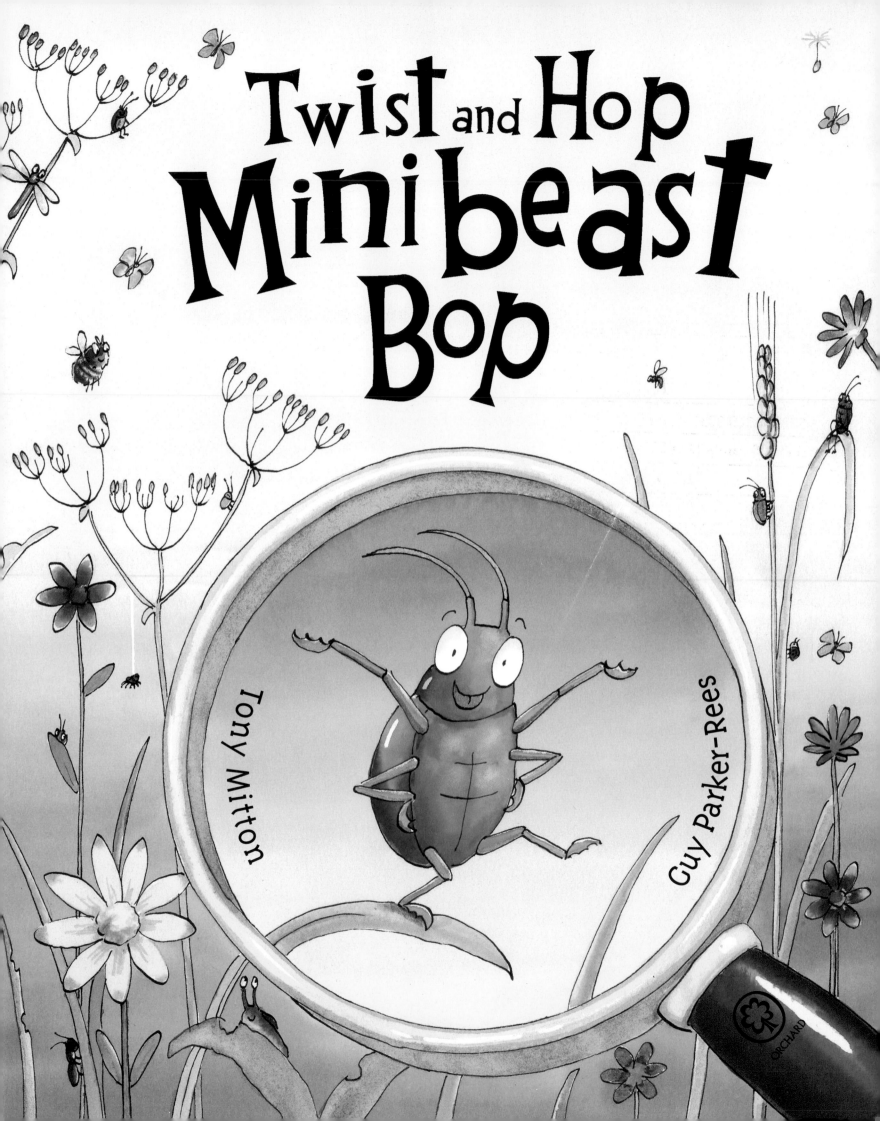

Twist and Hop Minibeast Bop

Tony Mitton

Guy Parker-Rees

Down by the woods, oh, come and see,

here in the stump of a fallen tree,

there's something strange that's made us stop . . .

Goodness me! It's a minibeast bop!

And, oh, what luck, it's just begun.

Let's crouch down here and watch the fun.

On come the ants
with slickety clicks.
How many legs does
each have? Six!

And here come the beetles,
looking SO FINE.
They've given their shells
a brilliant shine.

But poor old Snail. He'll miss the fun.

He set out late, and snails can't run.

He's feeling sad.

He'd love to go.

What a shame

that snails are slow.

The worms **wriggle up** so softly – listen . . .
And see how their silky skins can glisten!

The slugs slide on. They made good time.
They slithered here on gooey slime.

Says Snail, "I know I'm not so fast.
But maybe I'll get there at last."

The ladybirds turn every head.
They look so **bright**
in black and red.

But, jeepers creepers, look at this!

Did you ever see such ballgown bliss?

The butterfly frocks bring gasps and sighs.
Just see those colours and feast your eyes!

From way up there poor Snail looks down.

And then his face begins to frown.

He shrinks within his curly shell.

Is he sulking? Can we tell?

Do you hear the band begin to play?
The dancing's getting under way,
as minibeasts far too many to number
roll on doing the **wriggly rumba**.

Tiny piano and mini guitar
get them doing the cha-cha-cha.
Then as the rhythm comes alive,
everyone shakes to a jittery jive.

Beetles **boogie** and bugs go mad.

It's the **wildest** dance they've ever had.

But suddenly the music stops
as Bee Bandleader's baton drops.
In that hush they hear him shout,

"BOULDER COMING!
MAKE WAY!
LOOK OUT!"

And from the rim with a **RUMBLING** sound
comes a rolling rock that **SHAKES** the ground.

The minibeasts all look on with awe

as it grinds to a halt on the ballroom floor.

The beetles tremble. The insects wail.

But from the boulder . . .

"Pardon me for stopping the song,

but I simply had to roll along.

To slide down would have been too slow.

For then I might have missed the show."

Bee lifts his baton and gives a grin,
then says, "LET'S BOOGIE. Band, begin!"

The band pumps out a lively bop
which makes the minibeasts
wriggle and hop.

They JUMP and Jive,
they rave and
SHOUT.

Even the woodlice leap about.

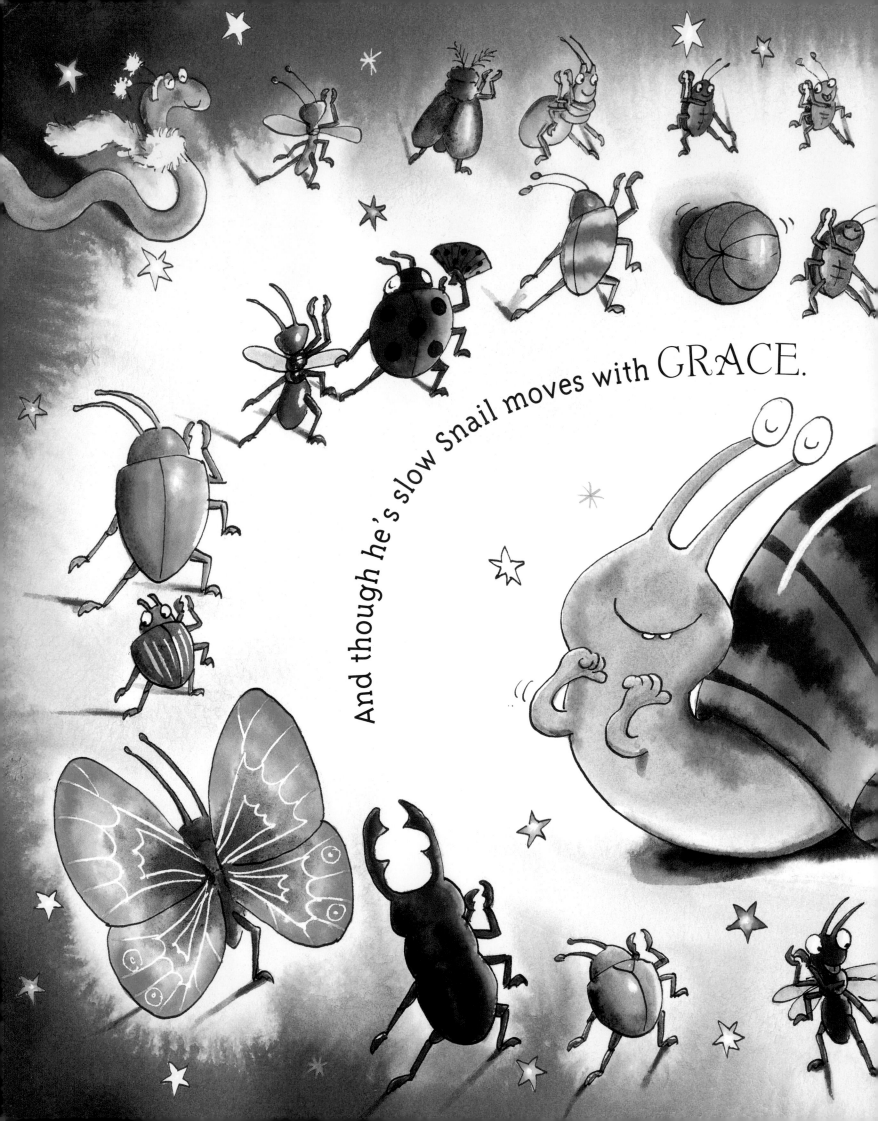

And though he's slow Snail moves with GRACE.

When it comes to gliding, he's an **ACE!**

The glow-worms glimmer their shimmering light as the minibeast bop hops on all night.